Teeny Tiny Tina
The Teeny Tiny Toothfairy

Written by Rosemary Evans

Illustrated by Erin Taylor

Teeny Tiny Tina the Teeny Tiny Tooth Fairy

Recipient of:

Mom's Choice Awards Gold Medal for Excellence in Children's Literature and the Royal Dragonfly Book Awards First Place.

Published by Wink Publishing - www.winkpublishing.com
Printed in China

Publisher's Cataloging-in-Publication Data

Evans, Rosemary R.
    Teeny tiny Tina the teeny tiny tooth fairy / written by Rosemary R. Evans ; illustrated by Erin Taylor.
        p. cm.
    ISBN: 978-1-4507-4721-9 (hardcover)
    ISBN: 978-0-9885976-0-0 (e-book)
    1.Tooth Fairy—Fiction. 2. Self-realization—Fiction. 3. Picture books for children.   I. Taylor, Erin, ill. II. Title. III. Series: Teeny tiny Tina.
    PZ7 .E89228 To 2013
    [Fic]—dc23   2011920600

"*Never underestimate the power of a strongly held dream. Only by dreaming do we turn our everyday lives into magical realities*"

-Rosemary Evans-

Dedicated to All the Tooth Fairies Everywhere

Once upon a time there was a teeny tiny fairy named Tina.

Teeny Tiny Tina wanted to be a tooth fairy more than anything else, but everyone told Tina that she was much too small to collect teeth.

Her sisters Annabelle and Rosebud got
to fly through the night and collect
all the beautiful little teeth.

Teeny Tiny Tina desperately
wanted to go with them.

"When will I grow?" Tina asked her mother, who was stringing popcorn for the birds.

"Be patient, little one, you will grow soon enough," explained Tina's mother.

But Tina didn't feel patient, and besides she needed a tiny tooth to sit by her dressing table in her bedroom, and she wanted to go and find it herself.

She sat on her bed to think. "Maybe if I ate more food, then I would get bigger," thought Tina. "Oh, but what if I just grow sideways and get so big and fat that my little fairy wings will not hold me up."

That was not a good thought.

Then Tina remembered what all that sugar would do to her teeny, tiny teeth, and decided that was not a very good idea!

So, Teeny Tiny Tina thought some more. "Oh, I know! I will put my little feet under a twig and have Rosebud and Annabelle pull on my arms and stretch me." Tina thought about that some more and decided that would make her arms all tingly and wouldn't help at all. Besides, her sisters might enjoy doing that a little too much!

So, Teeny Tiny Tina thought some more, and as she was deep in thought, she heard a faint knocking on her bedroom door.

"Who is it?" said Tina. "It's us," said Rosebud and Annabelle, "can we come in?" The door opened and there stood her older sisters.

"Tina, we need your help" said Rosebud and Annabelle. "A little girl has lost her tiny little baby tooth and we need to go get it but she didn't leave the door open and we can't get in."

"I tried to squeeze under the window, but I was too big!" said Rosebud.

"I tried to go in under the door,
but I was too tall!" said Annabelle.

"How can I help?" said Tina. "Oh", said Rosebud, "you can go through the keyhole and get into the bedroom. You will fit, because you are teeny. You will be able to go right through the little keyhole, pick up the tooth and fly back out."Teeny Tiny Tina was so happy that she could help. At last she was going to be a real tooth fairy!

So off they flew through the night, the three little sisters, holding hands. "Oh, this is so fun" exclaimed Tina!

When they got to the door of the little sleeping girl, Rosebud and
Annabelle said to Tina "There is the door. Now all you have to do is
fly right through that little key hole and find the tooth." So off Tina
flew, right through that tiny little key hole.

"Oh!" exclaimed Tina excitedly, when she found the beautiful, little tooth. "This is exactly what I need for a little stool to sit by my dressing table!"
As she picked up the tooth, a shiny coin magically appeared in its place.

When she came back out of the keyhole, she asked Rosebud and Annabelle, "Can I keep it?" "Of course you can" said her sisters, "after all you were the one that found it."

Tina could hardly wait to get home and put the tiny little tooth next to her dressing table. She was also excited to share the news with her mother, that she was indeed a real, honest to goodness tooth fairy.

"Look mom", Teeny Tiny Tina shouted, "I am a real Tooth Fairy. I got my first tooth." "Hooray for Tina," exclaimed her mother, "you are such a big helper and you are now officially a tooth fairy!"

Teeny Tiny Tina placed the tiny little tooth by her dressing table and sat on it. "This is such a beautiful little tooth; it is so perfect, and just the right size", exclaimed Tina!

As Teeny Tiny Tina looked in the tiny mirror, she thought: "I don't need to wish to be bigger, because just like my tiny little tooth, I am just the right size."

Teeny Tiny Tina learned that you can always be helpful, no matter your size, and she was now so happy to be called Teeny Tiny Tina the Teeny Tiny Tooth Fairy.

So remember:
It doesn't matter if you're short or tall,
It doesn't matter if you're big or small,
What matters most when the day is done;
Is, if along the way, you've helped someone.

So let your light shine and do your best,
Acknowledge your value and continue your quest,
Go after your dreams and never retreat,
Be nice and be helpful to all those you meet.

Then others will see you and know it is true,
When you help others, it also helps you.

Rosemary Evans lives in Lake Oswego, Oregon with her husband Richard. She is the mother of 4 children, and grandmother of 14.

She has written 4 children's books:

"The Little Princesses Magical Party", inspired by her three granddaughters. "Abrielle and Annelise stayed overnight, and we were having so much fun that they almost missed their bedtime story." Rosemary promised the girls that she would tell them a story, if they stayed in bed, left the lights off, and were very quiet. So she made up a story about two little princesses who had a magical party and learned what it really means to be a true princess.

"The Adventures of the Little Prince", inspired by her 11 grandsons. This story is about a young prince who wants to have a grand adventure, more than learning how to be a king. Very early one morning, he leaves the castle and sets off on his first adventure. On the way, he meets gypsies, a 'witch' who is really a lonely old lady, a young maiden who needs help, and a man whose horse has run away. The young prince finds many opportunities to help others and discovers that he has the qualities to become a great king after all.

"Teeny Tiny Tina the Teeny Tiny Tooth Fairy" One of Rosemary's granddaughters told her that when a tooth comes out and you leave it for the tooth fairy, she leaves you money. It inspired the author to write her first story about Teeny Tiny Tina, a cute little fairy who really, really wanted to be a tooth fairy, but everyone told her she was too teeny. You will enjoy discovering how Tina finally becomes a tooth fairy, in this wonderful, fun book.

"Teeny Tiny Tina and Her Teeny Tiny Pet" In this second Tina book you can read about Tina and her favorite pet named Kat. Tina's sisters Annabelle and Rosebud tell her that her pet is going to change into a butterfly. She goes to great lengths to try to stop the process. What happens to Kat? How does Tina discover that change is not something to fear? Read all about her adventures with Kat in this fun new book.

Her children's books can be ordered from Wink Publishing, by sending an email to **info@winkpublishing.com** or on Tina's website, **www.TinaToothFairy.com**. They will soon be available at major bookstores across the country.

Erin Taylor is a freelance illustrator who loves to draw, visit the zoo and travel. When she isn't on an airplane she can be found painting away with her husband Adam. To see more of her work, or to contact her about illustrating your next book, visit **www.ErinTaylorIllustrator.com**. Rosemary says "I am thrilled that my illustrator captured all four of my stories exactly as I envisioned them."

Rosemary is also the author of:

"Live Your Perfect Weight – The Missing Link to Weight Loss"
"Healthy Body – Healthy Skin"
"Change Your Script and Change Your Life"

You can order these three books at **www.LiveYourPerfectWeight.**